This Book Belongs to:

....

Bedtime Stories

Featuring The Fisherman and his Wife, The Bee Wing Ballgown & The Six Swans

igloo

The Fisherman & His Wife

There was once a poor fisherman who lived with his wife in a hovel near the sea. One day, he caught a huge fish. The fish said, "Have mercy, sir, let me live! I'm not really a fish at all, but an enchanted prince. I beg you, let me go!" The fisherman gasped in surprise, but he did as the fish asked.

When the fisherman returned home he told his wife all about it "And you asked for no reward in return for his life?" asked the wife. "Go back and tell the fish we want to live in a snug little cottage."

The fisherman went to the seashore, where the water was calm and blue, and said:

"O great fish in the sea!
My wife claims a reward from thee!"

The great fish appeared and said, "Well, fisherman, what does your wife desire?"

"My wife doesn't want to live in a hovel she wishes for a snug little cottage instead."

"Go home, then," said the fish. "She is in the cottage already!"

So the fisherman went home, and in place of the hovel was a snug little cottage.

"Is this not better than the pigsty?" she asked. And the fisherman had to agree that indeed it was better.

"Now, we shall be happy!" he said.

And so they lived happily for a few weeks, and then one day the wife said, "Husband, there is not enough room in this cottage.
I should like to have a large castle to live in. Go back to the fish and tell him we'd like a castle to live in instead."

The fisherman went to the seashore, where the sea looked sickly yellow and green. He stood at the water's edge and said:

      "O great fish in the sea!
      My wife claims a reward from thee."

"Well, what does she want now?" asked the fish.
"My wife wants a large stone castle now."
"Go home, then," said the fish. "She is in the castle already!"
So the fisherman went home. In place of the snug cottage was a large stone castle.

The wife said, "Is this not fine?" The fisherman agreed.

"Now we shall be happy."

The next morning, the fisherman was woken early by his wife, who said, "Husband, look outside the window. I should like to be Queen of all that land. Go back to the fish and tell him I'd like to be Queen."

So the fisherman went to the seashore, where the sea was dark and muddy, and the surface was broken by large waves. He stood a little way back from the water's edge and called:

"O great fish in the sea!
My wife claims a reward from thee."

"Well, what does she want now?" asked the fish.
"Oh!' said the fisherman. "My wife wishes to be Queen of the land as well."

"Go home, then," said the fish. "She is Queen already!"

So the fisherman went home, and as he approached the castle he saw that it was guarded by a troop of soldiers, and inside he saw his wife sitting on a golden throne with a crown of rubies upon her head. And his wife said, "I am Queen. Is it not great to be Queen?"

And the fisherman had to agree, and said, "Now we shall be happy!"

But the wife had not been Queen for more than an hour before she said to the fisherman: "Husband, it is not enough to be Queen, so I wish to be Empress as well. Go back to the fish."

The fisherman really didn't want to ask for yet another reward, but now his wife was Queen, so he couldn't refuse. So he went to the seashore, where the sea was black and full of violent waves. He stood quite a way back from the water's edge and cried:

> "O great fish in the sea!
> My wife claims a reward from thee!"

> "Well, what does she want now?" asked the fish.
> "Oh!" said the fisherman. "My wife wants to be
> the Empress as well."
> "Go home, then," said the fish. "She is the
> Empress already!"

So the fisherman went home once again, and as he walked up the red carpet in the great hall he saw his wife sitting on a huge throne, with a cloak of mink around her shoulders. And the wife said, "I am Empress. Is it not tremendous?"

And the fisherman had to agree that indeed it was tremendous to be Empress, and said, "Now, we shall be happy!"

But that night the fisherman's wife could not sleep. "For all my powers," she thought, "I do not have the power to make the sun rise in the sky." So she woke her husband to speak with him. She said, "Husband, go to the fish once more and tell him I must be lord of the sun and the moon."

The fisherman went to the seashore, where he saw that the waves were as tall as mountains and threatened to sweep him into the sea. And so he stood far from the water's edge, and shouted:

"O great fish in the sea!
My wife claims a reward from thee!"

"Well, what does she want now?" asked the fish.
"Oh!" said the fisherman. "My wife wishes to be lord of the sun and the moon."
"Go home, then," said the fish, who had finally had enough. "You'll find that it is a hovel again!"

And there they live to this very day.

The Bee Wing Ball Gown

O ne day, Paula walked home with her best friend, Yasmin and Yasmin's mum. They read the school newsletter. Paula gasped.

"Have you seen this?" she said, waving the newsletter in the air. "'This year's play is Cinderella,'" she read. "'Come and paint scenery or make up a song. Or take part in our competition to design Cinderella's ball gown. The winning design will become a real dress for the play!'" Yasmin and Paula hugged each other.
"I've got loads of ideas," said Paula, eyes shining.

At school the next morning, Paula fidgeted. At last it was time for Mrs. Frazer to read the school news.
"There's a meeting next Wednesday for all Cinderella actors and scenery makers. And the ball gown competition is now open for entries. We can only accept entries if you work with a partner."
"Yippee!" whispered Yasmin.

There were lots of questions, but Paula didn't hear them.
There was no chance that Mrs. Frazer would let her work with
Yasmin. Yasmin grabbed Paula's hand.
"Maybe we can swap partners," she whispered.

After lunch, Mrs. Frazer announced the pairs.
"Yasmin," said Mrs. Frazer. "You're with Maya."
Yasmin grinned. Maya loved drawing. She once won a
competition for her artwork, so she would be a great help.
"And Paula . . . " Mrs. Frazer consulted her list. "You're with Josie."

Josie? The new girl who never wore dresses and only liked bugs?
Paula tried to smile at Josie, but Josie was staring at her desk.
Paula turned to Yasmin, but her best friend was
chatting excitedly to Maya. Suddenly Paula
felt very alone.

That evening, Paula pulled her old fairytale books from her shelf.
She copied some gowns, carefully adding collars and bows, trying
out different shades and patterns. She spread the drawings across the
kitchen table.

"Very impressive," said Dad. "They could win any competition."

"I can't use them," Paula complained. "My partner's Josie and she's
bound not to like anything this girly."

"Well," soothed Dad, sitting down next to her, "no point starting over
if you already have something to work with."

"You're right!" Paula added a pink cloak with a furry hem to a ruffled
gown. "Josie won't mind if I do most of the work. Then she won't have
to do something she hates."

At break the next morning, Paula spotted Josie crouched by a bush.
Paula crouched down beside her.

"Ssh," said Josie. "See that ladybug? I don't want to disturb it."

Paula pulled out her drawings.
"Josie, I know you're not really into fashion design. These are for
the competition. You pick one and I can enter it for both of us."
The ladybug clambered onto a leaf and flew away. Josie looked through
the pictures and handed them back.

"Do you like them?" asked Paula nervously. Josie shook her head.
"Why?" Paula demanded.
"They're just . . . well . . . boring," said Josie quietly.
Paula's eyes prickled. She stuffed the pictures back in her bag, not
caring if they wrinkled or tore. "Well, you're boring too! All you're
interested in is bugs!"
Just after supper, Paula's doorbell rang and she heard the mumble
of voices.

"Paula?" called her mother.

The woman at the door was tall, with curly hair and a friendly smile. "I'm Josie's mother," she said. "I heard you two had an argument. Would you like to come over for an hour or so?"

Paula hesitated.
"You could still win that competition," Paula's mother reminded her.

Josie lived on the sixth floor of a tall building on a busy street. The door opened and Paula stepped into a room that smelled of hot sugar. "We're trying out a new popcorn machine," said Josie. "We can have some later."

Josie pushed open a door. "This is my bedroom."
When Josie's mum brought in the popcorn, the girls were poring over Josie's drawing book.
"Do you copy these from pictures?" Paula was asking.
"Sometimes I watch the insects in the park," said Josie. "And my cousin's got a wormery. You can see the worms moving inside."

Paula stroked a drawing of a bee's wing."It's like lace,'" she said. "I can't believe you can draw like this."

The final day of the competition arrived. Paula and Josie examined the display. There were about twenty ball gowns. Many had long puffy skirts. Some were decorated with cloaks, others with jewel-encrusted belts. Yasmin's and Maya's was a sweeping gown of gold cloth with scarlet shoes and a sparkly headband.

Paula and Josie's design was nothing like the others. It had red shoes with black spots, leggings as green as a cricket and a shiny, beetle-black top. A floor-length lacy wing fell from each shoulder.

The outfit was completed by a pink hat.

"Cinderella's got a worm on her head!" laughed a little boy.

Mrs. Frazer arrived with a man that the children had never seen before. "Mr. Lee is helping me judge," she said. "He designs costumes for films and plays."
The judges examined every picture, whispered together and wrote some notes. Finally, Mr. Lee stepped forward.
"We have a winner," he said. The girls held their breath.
"We loved them all." He paused. "But the winner is . . . Yasmin and Maya."

Yasmin and Maya grinned as everybody clapped. Josie turned to Paula.
"I bet you wish Yasmin was your partner," she said.
"No!" Paula was surprised. "I'm really glad we've become friends."

"Josie? Paula?" Mrs. Frazer beckoned. Mr. Lee was holding their picture. "This is very different," he said. "Not quite right for Cinderella. But it's perfect for the Carnival Queen Bee leading our procession this year. Can we use it?"

"Yes, please," gasped the girls.

"And you two can ride on the Carnival float," said Mrs. Frazer.

Josie and Paula looked at each other.

"Thank you," said Josie. Paula grinned and clasped Josie's hand. They might not have won the school competition but they were to be in the carnival parade!

It couldn't be a better prize!

The Six Swans

Once upon a time, there lived a King who had one daughter and six sons. The King loved his children very much, for his wife had died many years earlier and they were the only relations he had left in the world.

One day, the King went hunting. He rode deeper and deeper into the woods following a stag, until all at once he realized he was lost. Each way he turned the paths looked the same. He grew more and more worried until suddenly he spotted an old woman sitting on a tree trunk. "Excuse me," said the King politely. "Could you show me the way out of the woods so I can find my way home?"

The woman saw his royal robes and realized he was a King.
"I will show you on one condition," she answered slyly. "You must marry my beautiful daughter and take her to be Queen of your land."
"And what if I do not care to take the hand of your daughter?" asked the King.
"Then I will leave you alone for the wild animals to hunt!" she replied.

The King was worried about his children, so he was forced to agree.

The next day the King kept his word and married the woman's daughter. But he saw that she would not be a kind stepmother to his children, so he asked his servants to hide his family in a castle, deep in the oak forest.

Every morning, before the sun rose, the King left his wife sleeping and went to visit his children.

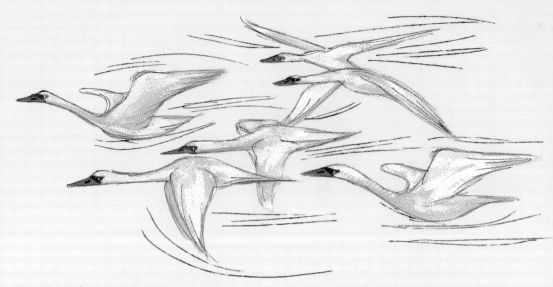

One day, however, his wife woke early and noticed that he was gone. The same thing happened the next morning. She became suspicious and decided to follow him.

On seeing that he had seven children hiding in a castle, the Queen became very angry. She took a ball of magic string and, using a spell, turned the string into magic shirts made of pure white silk.

The next time the King went out hunting, the evil Queen hurried to the castle in the oak forest. Thinking it was their father arriving, the six boys rushed outside to greet him. Immediately, the Queen threw the magic shirts over them. At once, the six boys were turned into six white swans, and all flew away.

When the King went to visit his children the next morning, only his daughter remained.
"You must stay here until I can find a new, safe place to hide you," he told her.

That night, as the winds howled, the daughter was sure she heard her brothers calling in the forest, so she left the castle to look for them.

All night she searched and searched, until she could go no further.
At last she spotted a hut.
"Maybe I can shelter here," she thought, opening the door.

Inside she saw six beds. She longed to lie down, but she was worried
that the owners might return, so she hid herself under one and closed
her eyes to sleep.

The girl was woken by the sound of beating wings. Opening her eyes,
she was amazed to see six swans land on the beds. As each landed, its
feathers fell off, revealing her six handsome young brothers.

"My brothers!" she cried, climbing out from under the bed.

"You must not stay here," they told her. "We cannot protect you, for we are only human for a few moments each day before we turn back into swans."

"There must be something I can do to help?" said their sister. "There is," replied her oldest brother, "but it will not be easy. For six years you must not speak or laugh. And in your solitude you must sew six shirts made of the tiniest flower petals."

At once, their sister set off in search of the tiniest flowers she could find. Her search took her to another kingdom, where a carpet of the daintiest flowers grew on the forest floor. There she sat down and began to sew.

The next day the King of the land passed by.

"What are you sewing with my prettiest flowers?" he questioned. But the girl could not speak, of course, so she just kept on sewing.

The King was enchanted by this beautiful silent girl and fell in love with her. Before the summer was over, he had persuaded her to marry him, even though she had never spoken a word.

The King's mother did not like this new, silent girl. After the girl gave birth to the King's first child, the mother stole the baby and spread lies that the girl had given it away. The King, who loved his wife, refused to believe the lies.

When the young Queen had another child and it too went missing, the evil mother demanded that her son take action.

"My wife wants to do nothing more than sew all day long, every day," he thought. "Perhaps my mother is right about her."

The King asked to see the Queen the next day. All through the night she sewed. By morning she had finished the six shirts, except for the last sleeve of one.

As the Queen stood before the King, there was the noise of beating wings. The Queen threw the petal shirts over the swans' heads and the spell was finally broken. Before her stood her six brothers, one with a wing of a swan as an arm, for it was that shirt she had not finished in time.

"At last I can speak!" she cried. When the King learned what his mother had done, he sent her away forever. The six brothers took it upon themselves to find their missing nieces and nephews. The King was so grateful he invited his wife's brothers to live with them, for their father had passed away in the six years gone.

And so it was that the King, Queen, their children and the six brothers all lived together in happiness for the rest of their lives.